LOOK AROUND!
A Book About Shapes

LOOK AROUND!

A Book About Shapes

BY LEONARD EVERETT FISHER

Puffin Books

The artwork was painted with acrylics on textured paper.

PUFFIN BOOKS
Published by the Penguin Group
Viking Penguin Inc., 40 West 23rd Street, New York, New York 10010, U.S.A.
Penguin Books Ltd, 27 Wrights Lane, London W8 5TZ, England
Penguin Books Australia Ltd, Ringwood, Victoria, Australia
Penguin Books Canada Ltd, 2801 John Street, Markham, Ontario, Canada L3R 1B4
Penguin Books (N.Z.) Ltd, 182–190 Wairau Road, Auckland 10, New Zealand

Penguin Books Ltd, Registered Offices: Harmondsworth, Middlesex, England

First published in the United States of America by Viking Penguin Inc., 1987
Published in Picture Puffins, 1989
10 9 8 7 6 5 4 3 2 1
Copyright © Leonard Everett Fisher, 1987
All rights reserved
LIBRARY OF CONGRESS CATALOGING IN PUBLICATION DATA
Fisher, Leonard Everett.
   Look around! : a book about shapes / by Leonard Everett Fisher   p.   cm.
   Reprint. Originally published: New York, N.Y. : Viking Kestrel, 1987.
Summary: Presents basic geometrical shapes in familiar scenes for the reader to identify.
ISBN 0-14-050572-5
1. Geometry—Juvenile literature. [1. Geometry. 2. Shape.]   I. Title.
QA445.5.F57 1989   516.2—dc19   88–29801   CIP   AC

Printed in Japan by Dai Nippon Printing Co. Ltd.
Set in Bembo

For Elizabeth and Susan

CIRCLE

A circle is a round shape.
It has no beginning.
It has no end.
The center is always as
far from one edge of
the circle as it is
from another.

Can you find these shapes on the next page?

Which shape is not a circle?

SQUARE

A square has four
straight sides.
All the sides are the
same size.

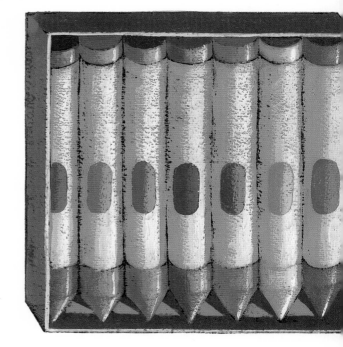

Can you find these shapes on the next page?

Are all the shapes squares?

RECTANGLE

A rectangle has four straight sides.
The top and bottom are one size.
The left and right sides are another size.

BOXES!
BOXES!
Leonard Everett Fisher

Be My Valentine

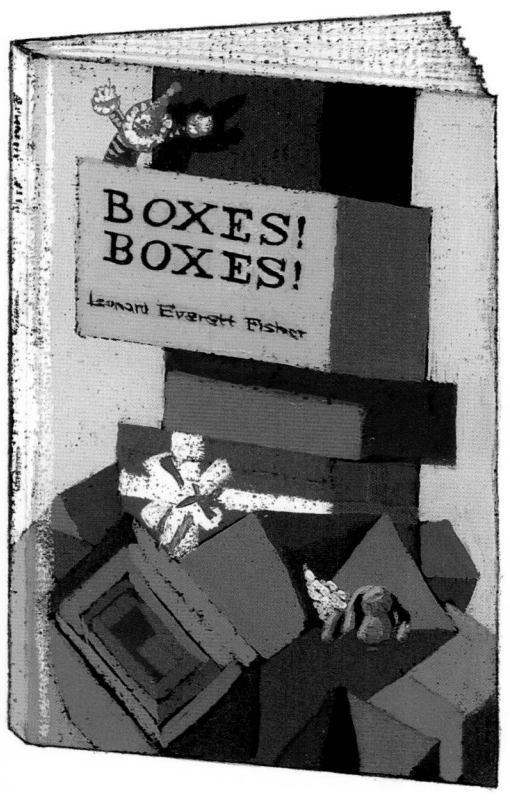

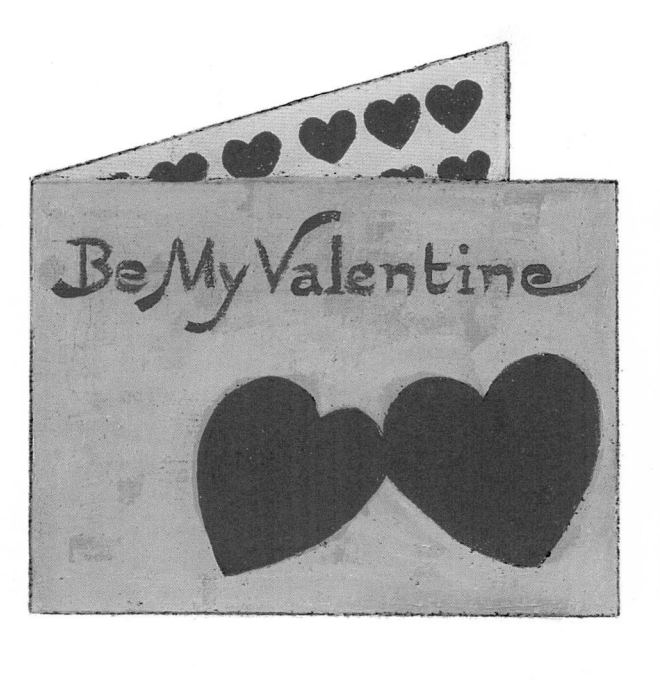

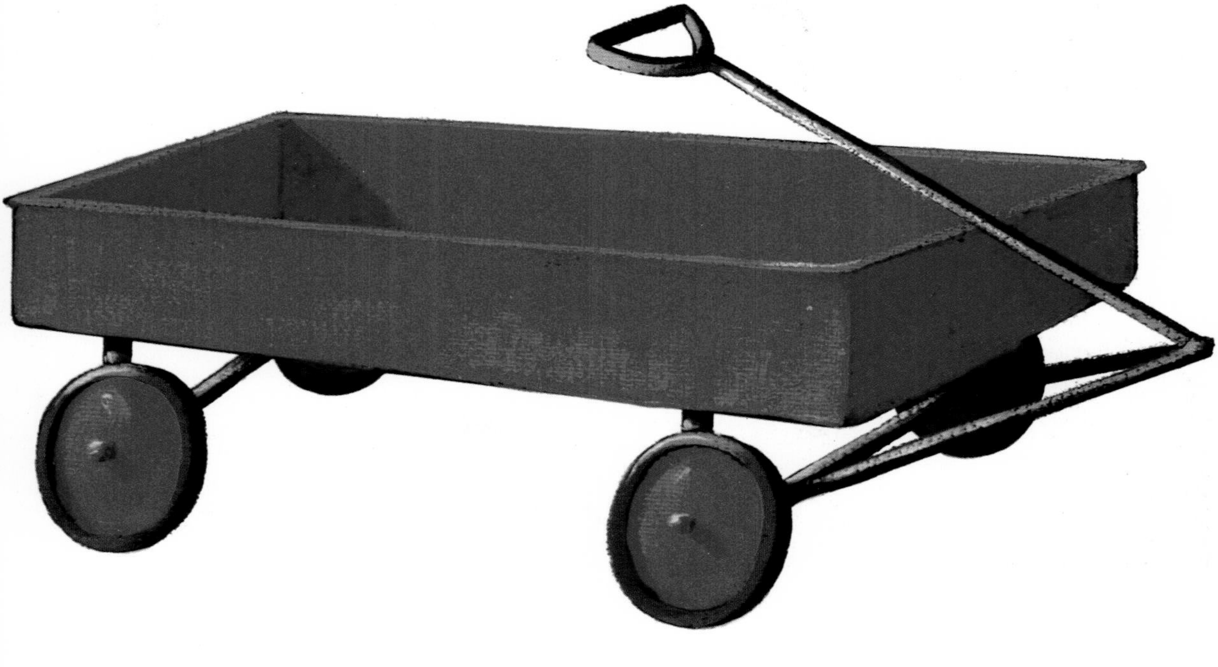

Can you find these shapes on the next page?

Which ones are not rectangles?

TRIANGLE

A triangle has three straight sides. Sometimes the sides are the same size. Sometimes they are not.

Can you find these shapes on the next page?

Are they all triangles?

LOOK AROUND!

Can you find things that are a ●

or a ■ , a ▮ , or a ▲ ?

A  has squares all over it.

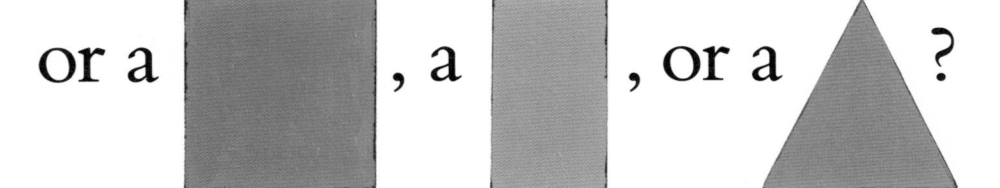 are rectangles with squares and circles.

A  wears a in the shape of a triangle.

A  is made up of circles and a triangle.

A STOP is an octagon.

And a  is shaped like a heart.

LOOK AROUND!

More Shapes

diamond

pentagon

heart

octagon

oval

parallelogram

crescent

hexagon

star